The Great Kachina

by Lou Bader
illustrated by Mary Toerner

Copyright © 1996 by Lou Bader

All rights reserved. No part of this book may be used or reproduced in any manner whatsoever without prior written permission from the publisher except in the case of brief quotations in critical reviews and articles.

ISBN 0-929385-60-8

Cover art and illustrations by
Mary Toerner

Published by

StarChild Press
A division of
Light Technology Publishing
P.O. Box 1526
Sedona, AZ 86339

Printed by
MISSION POSSIBLE
Commercial Printing
P.O. Box 1495
Sedona, AZ 86339

The Great
Kachina

Sandy was just letting the world know he was up.

1t was very early in the morning. The moon was still shining brightly over Wing Mountain. All was quiet. You could hear a pine cone drop on the soft carpet of pine needles. Up at the top of a large Ponderosa Pine tree, Sandy the saucy Abert Squirrel, with his perky tufted ears, had just emerged from his nest, and for no reason at all was scolding the world. He really wasn't unhappy. It was just his way of letting the world know that he was up, and therefore everyone else should rise.

Matilda, the Cottontail Rabbit nesting way back in a drift of pine logs, thought to herself, "There he goes again, showing off." But she was too happy and too busy to be much concerned about Sandy, because snuggling up close to her warm fur were five little newborn babies. This was her first litter, and she was very proud and thought that they were beautiful.

Now, some of us, if we could have seen them, might not have thought they were so pretty. Their eyes were closed and their pink little bodies had not a single hair. They were as naked as could be.

Several days before the little bunnies were born, Matilda would pull her fur out from her soft underside. This did not cause her any discomfort because nature allowed this fur to be special and easy to pull out at this time. She kept pulling out her fur until she had made the most wonderful nest.

Now, as Matilda lay there with her warm brood, she was content; she had just had a nice breakfast of fresh new grass. It was spring and the grass was light green and very nutritious. This was one of the

reasons she had decided to have her babies at this time of the year.

All of a sudden she heard a distressing sound, a little *squeak-squeak*. Turning her head she saw that one of the little bunnies had managed to fall out of the nest and was yelling his head off. Reaching over with her chin, she shoved him back into the warm fur, and without another peep he started to nurse.

Matilda shook her head and said, "I'm going to name you Jasper. I hope this is not a sign that you are going to get into a lot of trouble when you grow up."

Little did she know! Little did she know!

That evening after Old Sol the sun had gone down behind Wing Mountain, Matilda began to feel the pangs of hunger. After all, she was feeding five little bunnies. She was thinking about that nice patch of grass she had discovered. It made her mouth water. She decided to peek out to see if it were safe to leave. But first she had to warn the babies to keep very quiet while she was gone. This was the first lesson they would need to learn.

"Do not make a sound when I leave, because Slinky the Badger is around and there is nothing he would like better than to have a dinner of baby rabbits," Matilda told them.

Matilda hated to scare the baby bunnies but she knew that it was necessary if she was to secure their safety. When she arrived at the entrance of the drift, her nose began to go up and down, sniff, sniff, very swiftly. She was checking the air for a scent of Slinky the Badger. Not catching the scent

Matilda was very proud
of her five little newborn bunnies.

Slinky the Badger was lying up against a rock.

of any danger, she cautiously poked her head out and looked around. Suddenly she saw a brown shape lying up against a rock. It was lying so flat that she might have thought it was part of the rock. But she was too wise. She knew that it was Slinky the Badger. She hurried back to her nest as fast as she could.

When Matilda arrived she saw that Jasper had his head up and was about to sneeze. Quickly she placed her paw over his mouth and quietly said, "God bless you."

Matilda told Jasper, "You must learn to control all such noises."

Jasper's thoughts were that there sure is a lot to learn in this big world.

Later in the evening Matilda decided to check again to see if it was safe to go to the Green Pasture. Sniffing and looking into every corner of the woods, she thought that it was all right to leave the drift.

As Matilda entered the Green Pasture she met Jacklyn the Jack Rabbit, who was really not a Rabbit but a Hare. She was there with her eight children. Her children were different from Matilda's. They were born with their eyes open and with their fur already grown. After a few days they could hop around as well as anyone and could eat grass.

After saying good morning, Matilda remarked, "How nice it is to have children who can take care of themselves so soon."

Jacklyn said, "Well, not really. You see, I have to watch them every minute to see that they do not stray away. Have you ever tried to keep an eye on eight little bunnies? I will be a nervous wreck by the time they are all grown. Your children are well hidden and safely away from most danger."

Matilda replied, "Well, it is the way the good Lord planned it and we can't do much about it, can we?"

So, after some more pleasantries they both went their ways. Matilda noticed how Jacklyn's children scampered into all directions, and said to herself, "I guess I'm really better off the way things are."

Heading back to the drift, Matilda heard a noise, and as she was always on the alert for danger, she dove behind a bush. Looking up, she saw Misty the Donkey. They had become fast friends. In fact it was Misty who told her about the Green Pasture. She laughed and said, "Hello, Misty. My goodness, whom do you have with you?"

Misty replied, "This is Niño, my baby, as you can plainly see. Isn't he beautiful?"

"Indeed he is," exclaimed Matilda. What lovely ears he has. But aren't his legs far too long for him?"

"Of course not," Misty said. It is a fact that baby donkeys, and horses, for that matter, have the lower part of their legs as long as they will ever be. By that, I can tell that Niño will be a nice big boy when he grows up."

Niño moved close to his mother and asked, "Will I ever get as big as Highness the Palomino?"

"Oh no. Burros never get as big as horses, but you will be a good size someday, so don't worry about it," his mother answered.

Matilda told Misty about her five babies and mentioned that one of them, the one that she had named Jasper, might get into a little trouble when he grew up.

Misty said, "Well, I know that Jasper and Niño will become good friends. When your bunnies are up and around we must get together so Niño and Jasper will have a chance to play."

Matilda said, "How nice," and they both went their ways, Misty back to the barn and Matilda to the drift.

Now, some time later, Jasper, who by now was partly grown, and Niño, about six months of age, happened to meet one day. This is what took place.

Niño, like all little donkeys, stayed close to his mother for the first few months that he was in this world. But he was feeling pretty independent one day so he thought he would go to the Green Pasture. However, as always, he kept his mother in his sight. He knew that if any trouble occurred he could call for help.

Walking into the Green Pasture, he noticed the most beautiful bunch of clover. It was nice and green, with some purple flowers in the middle. He thought, "Will that ever taste delicious!" Reaching out, he took a big bite. His jaws snapped together but the clover disappeared. He couldn't believe his eyes. One minute the clover was there and the next it was gone. He turned away, then looked back, and there was the clover. What in the world could this mean? He snapped as fast as he could, but the clover disappeared again.

Just then he heard someone laughing. It was more like a giggle. He heard a voice say, "What's the matter, you silly Burro? Here is your clover. I was just pulling it away to have a little fun."

At that moment Jasper came out of a rabbit hole and handed the clover to Niño.

Niño indignantly shouted, "What's the big idea? And who are you?"

"I know who *you* are! You're Niño," said Jasper. "How do I know that? Well, my mother Matilda

"Silly burro... here is your clover. I was just having fun!"

told me that if I ever saw anyone with ears bigger than mine, it would be you, Niño."

Niño laughed and said, "They are bigger than yours, but yours are just as pretty, and so pink on the underside."

Jasper liked Niño right off.

"How would you like to go play over by the creek?" Jasper asked. "It's lots of fun to run and slide on one side and land on the other."

Are you sure I won't slip and land in the creek?" Niño asked.

"Of course you won't," Jasper replied.

When they arrived at the creek, Jasper pointed out a slippery slide on the bank.

"You go way back and take a run, hit the slide and you will scoot over the creek," Jasper explained.

"Are you sure I won't fall into the creek?" Niño asked.

Jasper laughed and said, "Of course not. Would I try to fool you?"

"Why don't you go first and let me watch you so I can see how you do it?" Niño asked.

"Oh no," Jasper said, "that would take all the fun out of it. It is best that you do as I say."

"Okay," Niño said suspiciously.

He walked back from the creek and said, "Is this far enough?"

Jasper said, "Go back a little farther."

"How's this?" shouted Niño.

"Great. Start running," Jasper answered.

At that Niño ran as fast as he could. He hit the slide, went way up in the air and *kaplunk*, landed in the middle of the creek. When he crawled out he was wet from head to hoof. He saw Jasper doubled up in a fit of laughter, compulsively writhing on the ground.

"You did that on purpose," Niño said.

"No, I didn't. You just didn't get back far enough

to start your run," Jasper teased. "Do you want to try it again?"

"Absolutely not," Niño said. "I've heard about your mischievous tricks."

So that's how Niño and Jasper met. They soon became best friends.

One day Niño asked Jasper, "Where do you live?"

"Since I left home I found a wonderful place under some logs in the big forest," replied Jasper.

"Why do you live in such a funny place?" asked Niño. "Why don't you come and live in the barn with us?"

Jasper exclaimed, "Don't be silly. Live in the barn? Don't you know that Flat Cat lives there? I wouldn't want a thing to do with Flat Cat. She scares me with those long claws, and such awful teeth."

Niño said, "Have you heard that Flat Cat has been living with Papa Bader for two or three years now?"

"Well, I'm glad to hear that. Maybe tonight I will go over to the barn and look around," Jasper said.

That night when the moon came up, Jasper hopped out from under the old woodpile and headed toward the barn. He still wasn't quite sure about Flat Cat. But, well, if Niño said she was gone, he guessed she was gone. He came, hippity hop, up to the barn door and saw a little hole under the floor. He took a deep breath and scooted in. It was

nice and dry and comfortable there. Some sweet alfalfa leaves had fallen down through the cracks of the floor. He stopped to eat some.

"Golly," he thought, "this is wonderful. A nice warm place to make my nest, and lots of food to eat. I know that Niño and the horses will not mind if I eat a little of their hay and oats."

Just then he thought he saw a shadow over his shoulder. He shuddered a little because he was really afraid of cats and large dogs. He managed a little nervous laugh and said, "I have to watch myself or I will imagine I see all kinds of things."

Just then a large object jumped down in front of him. A huge rat with enormous yellow fangs hissed at him.

"Rabbit, what are you doing in my barn? Get out of here or I'll eat you alive," shouted the rat.

Jasper's little heart just about stopped.

"It really isn't your barn, sir," he said meekly in a small voice.

"Oh yeah?" yelled the rat. "Beat it or you won't see another day."

Trembling like a leaf, Jasper was about to run when he heard another voice, a well-modulated, refined, cultured voice.

"Oh, no you won't!"

Jasper turned around quickly and there was, of all people, Flat Cat.

"Oh dear," cried Jasper, "what will become of me? A mean rat in front of me, and Flat Cat behind, about to pounce on me. Oh me! Poor me! Poor me!!"

Just at that time Flat Cat let out a terrible scream,

A huge rat jumped in front of Jasper.

and sprang. Poor Jasper cringed down, expecting to feel her claws at any moment. But, what do you know, Flat Cat sprang right over Jasper and landed smack on the back of the mean old rat.

"You get out of this barn, you old rat fink, or I'll teach you a lesson that you'll never forget!" Flat Cat shouted at the rat.

The big rat heard this and, not being a dumb rat, beat a hasty retreat. The last he was seen, he was running down Hideaway Trail, yelling, "Let me out of here! Let me out of here!"

"Thank you, Flat Cat," Jasper said politely. "I guess I misjudged you."

Flat Cat, being a wise old cat, accepted Jasper's apology with a great deal of poise, and said to Jasper, "That's all right, but in the future don't make decisions about other people's character until you know them better."

Flat Cat turned away and, with a little smile on her face, walked slowly toward Papa's house.

Jasper knew that the mean old rat would never bother him again, and after making a nice nest he went out to tell Niño all about his adventures. However, after they had talked it over they felt sort of sorry for the rat. Even though he was grumpy and mean-looking, he was, after all, still one of God's creatures. They hoped he would find a hollow log and make a living in the forest.

One day while walking in the forest looking for green clover, Niño spied a very slow-moving creature strolling across the prairie. Niño said, "Look at that funny thing. What is it?"

Jasper said, "That's Quilliton the Porcupine. You see all those strange long things sticking out of his back and along his tail? They are quills. Even though he cannot throw them like a dart, he can slap you with his tail. If you get them in your nose or face it is very painful."

Niño said, "He doesn't look like he is so tough. Let's sneak up and frighten him."

Jasper warned, "I wouldn't do that if I were you."

"Come on, don't be chicken," Niño said. "I'm going to come up behind him and yell in his ear. I'd like to see him jump."

Now, Quilliton was half asleep as he crawled along, and he didn't see Niño coming up behind him. Finally, when Niño got as close as he could, he let out the loudest donkey bray he could manage.

Quilliton slapped with his tail. Niño saw it coming and pulled back, but not soon enough. Although he did not get the full attack of the tail, he did get several quills in his nose.

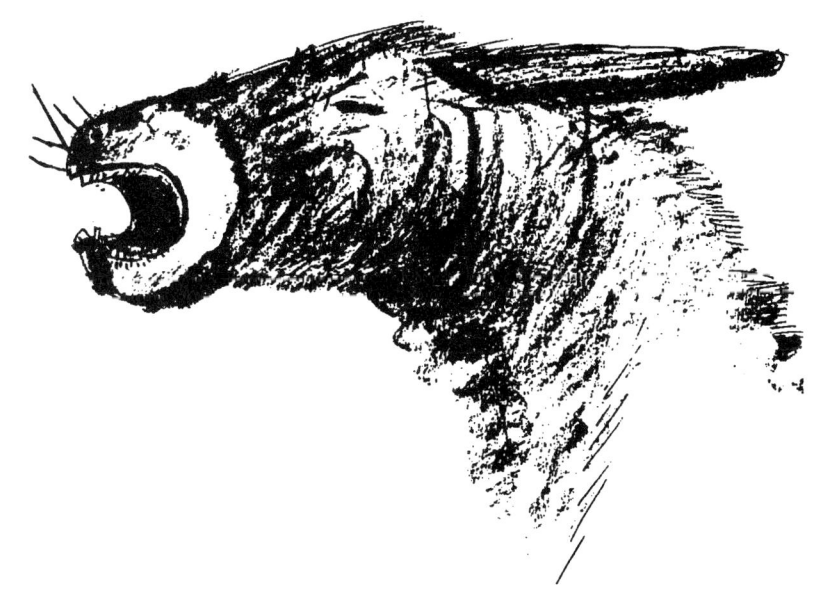

When he felt the sting and the pain of the barbs, he shouted, "What did you do that for? I was just having fun."

Quilliton said, "You shouldn't sneak up behind someone and yell, especially with such a raucous sound. You will never pass for a nightingale with that racket of a voice."

But when Quilliton saw how sad Niño was, he softened and said, "You had better go and have those things taken out of your nose. They can cause infection, and because of the barbs on them, they can work farther into your flesh. Now go to that human person that lives on your ranch and have him remove them."

"You shouldn't sneak up behind someone and yell."

"But before you go I have a message for you and the rest of the animals."

Holding back his tears, Niño asked, "What is the message?"

"It is just this," Quilliton answered in a mysterious voice. "While I was eating bark up in the San Francisco Peaks, I overheard the Great Kachina say that he was going to cause the Peaks to erupt into another volcano, that it had been two million eight hundred thousand years since it had exploded, and he was tired of people using his mountain for ski runs, building cabins there, and allowing sheep and cattle to graze there."

"So all of you had better consider a hasty retreat, or you will be covered with ashes, and that goes for your cat and dog, too."

Niño and Jasper hurried to tell Misty what had happened.

"Well, Quilliton is an old crab, and you can't believe half of what he says. But we'd better be careful and look into this anyway," Misty said with some concern in her voice.

"But first come with me over by the barn where Papa Bader is working. Stand near him and poke your nose up so he can notice your trouble."

When Papa Bader saw poor Niño's nose he said, "Come here, little fellow."

He took out a pair of snips and cut off the ends of the quills. This was to cause them to collapse. He quickly pulled out the quills. Niño jerked back every time one of the quills was removed. He thought, "I'll never do that again. This is the hard way to learn."

When Niño and Jasper went into detail about what Quilliton's warning had been all about, that The Great Kachina was going to cause the Peaks to erupt again, Misty said, "We must get the animals together for a meeting."

She appointed Jasper to tell all the animals in the woods. Niño was to alert the farm animals. All were supposed to meet in the Green Pasture at sun-up.

Quilliton spoke in a mysterious voice. "I have a message for you."

The next morning the animals all came on time. There was much chatter and talking back and forth. They were all very much alarmed and frightened.

Misty took charge and called the meeting to order.

"Be quiet!" Misty exclaimed. "This is serious business. We must decide what we must do."

After a great deal of time, Misty said, "I have heard all of your ideas. This is what I have decided. I will appoint a committee to go and talk to the Great Kachina. Do I have any volunteers?"

Jasper said, "I'll go."

Niño said, "Me too."

Herman the Duck quacked, "I'll go, if you don't walk too fast."

Bozo the big Hound Dog barked, "You will need some protection, so I'll go."

Sandy the Squirrel said, "You will need a lookout. I can climb trees, so you will need me."

Short the little Dog said, "Take me along."

Sandy snorted, "What could a tiny Dog like you do?"

Short said sharply, "I am the best barker on the whole ranch. You will need me to give the alarm in case we meet some Bears."

"Bears?" said Herman. "Are there Bears? Perhaps I'd better not go. I would just be in the way."

"No, too late," said Misty. "You're in this and can't back out."

The next morning Short went into the kitchen where Mama Bader was cooking breakfast. She kept dancing around, jumping up and down, turning circles and walking on her hind feet.

Mama Bader said, "Even though we can't communicate vocally, I can tell by your body language that you want something. What is it? Do you and the other animals want to go on a picnic in the woods?"

Short turned a back-flip.

"I thought so," said Mama Bader. "Do you want me to pack a lunch for you?"

Short barked a little series of yaps.

"Okay. Tell Bozo the Hound to come in and I will fill the backpack that he has learned to carry."

Short ran out to get Bozo while Mama Bader prepared a big picnic lunch. She put in some nice corn kernels for Herman the Duck, jelly and peanut butter sandwiches, some macaroon cookies, carrots and lettuce for Jasper, and some cashew nuts for Sandy. She even put in a large bone for Bozo and a bottle of Kool Aid and a little pan to pour it in. She knew that Sandy the Squirrel would know how to handle that. She also threw in some napkins, as she was a very neat lady and didn't want dirty paws and muzzles.

After loading up the pack on Bozo, they all quacked and squeaked and barked goodbye. Mama Bader admonished them not to go too far or stay away too long. They were now ready to go to see the Great Kachina.

Just at that time little Emma Jean came home from school. She was garbed in a pink pinafore dress. Her long curls were peeking out of a bonnet trimmed

Emma Jean rode home from school on her Pony Firefly.

with white lace, and she even had socks to match. Her patent leather shoes, with pearl buttons, were as shiny as could be. She didn't dress so fancy every

day, but today was dress-up day and all the girls and boys dressed as spiffy as they knew how.

After she tied up Firefly her Pony, who was her transportation to and from school, she went into the kitchen. When she saw Bozo with his pack she asked, "What are the animals up to?"

"Oh, they want to go on a picnic in the woods," Mama Bader said. "I have packed a lunch that Bozo will carry."

"How nice, Mama. Can I go with them? Tomorrow is Saturday, and I can do my homework on Sunday. I would so much love to have a trip in the forest. All the wildflowers are blooming now, and it would be so much fun. I would even have Bozo to protect me. I'll take my sleeping bag, Mama. Please let me go, please, Mama!"

"All right," Mama Bader said, "but take a warm shirt and jacket."

When this was all completed she gave Emma Jean a big kiss, and off they all went on their big adventure.

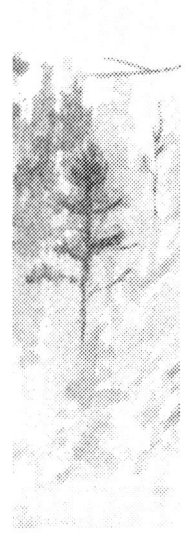

Now, there was something that no one else knew but Emma Jean, and that was the fact that she could really talk to the animals. So, when they were out of hearing distance, she turned to Niño and said, "Now what is this all about? Picnic indeed! What are you up to? Out with it!"

Niño tried to relate the warning that Quilliton had given, that the San Francisco Peaks were about to blow up again. The animals all tried to talk at once. Emma Jean said, "Please be quiet. Let Niño tell me all about it."

After she had gotten the gist of the story she said, "Come on, we must seek out the Great Kachina. We have no time to lose. I must be home by Sunday evening."

Off they went in a fast walk, Herman the Duck trailing after. By noon they had traveled about half-way up the mountain.

Herman said, "Please stop and rest. Besides, I am starved."

Emma Jean took the pack off Bozo and spread a tablecloth out on the grass. They all sat around and enjoyed the sandwiches and other good things.

"We must stop eating and save some of our food for tomorrow," said Emma Jean.

She had started to put the food back in the backpack when she heard a gruff voice say, "Not so fast, little girl. I haven't eaten yet." Out of the bushes came the biggest Black Bear anyone could imagine.

Short sprang up between the basket and the Bear, barking furiously, "Get back, you big bum, or I'll bite you."

"Ho! Ho! Ho!" laughed the Bear. "What could a little Dog like you do? Stand back or I'll slap you silly."

Bozo began to growl. The hair on his back stood up and his lip curled to expose his nice, long teeth. He rushed forward, but the Bear, rising up on his hind feet, slapped Bozo, throwing him up against a tree and knocking the breath out of him. By that time Short was behind the Bear and he grabbed hold of the Bear's stubby tail.

The Bear turned in sharp circles, trying to slap Short, but he could not reach her. No matter how fast he circled, Short hung on. By that time Bozo had regained his breath, and he dashed in and grabbed the Bear by the ear. This proved too much for the Bear. He headed out, with Short still hanging on to his tail.

Out of the bushes came the biggest Black Bear anyone could imagine.

Emma Jean yelled, "Short, let go!" Short let go and went sailing into Emma Jean's arms. All the animals gathered around Short and told her how brave she was.

Short said, "Shucks, it wasn't anything that any red-blooded American Dog wouldn't do." But inside she really felt proud.

Emma Jean said, "We must move on so we can make camp before dark. The Great Kachina lives just below Humphreys Peak; we will set up there."

When they arrived they began to make a comfortable camp. Herman the Duck gathered some grass for a nice nest. Sandy the Squirrel found a crook in a tree branch. Jasper saw a dandy spot under a log.

Niño said, "I'll just lie down on some soft grass."

Emma Jean stretched out her sleeping bag.

Short said, "I'll just curl up with Emma Jean on the foot of her sleeping bag." So, after some more sandwiches and other goodies, they all turned in for a night's sleep.

But Bozo, the big Hound, decided to keep an eye open and to stay awake. It wasn't long before he heard a strange noise. It was weird. It sounded like the wind. It went "Woo-woo." Bozo raised his ears up so he could hear better. The noise grew louder and louder, and all of a sudden there was a great stroke of lightning and crashing thunder.

Emma Jean and all the animals awakened. Short dove into the sleeping bag with only his little black nose sticking out. Everyone else jumped to their feet.

They heard a voice say, "I am the Great Kachina. Who is it that dares to come to my mountain and sleep at the foot of my personal Peak? Speak or I'll bring some more lightning."

Emma Jean spoke up. "We are friends, Great Kachina, sir. We have come with a petition for you, a request that you do not allow the Peaks to erupt again."

"Silence!" shouted The Great Kachina.

"Ha, ha, ha," laughed the Great Kachina. "Why do you think I would listen to a little girl and such a funny bunch of animals? But on second thought, I will consider your request. First you must fulfill a quest I will give you."

Emma Jean said, "Yes indeed, we will. Tell us, what is your wish?"

The Great Kachina said, "It won't be easy. There are certain things I need in order to perform my special magic. I require first of all some hair from Terror the Mountain Lion's tail."

She spoke up. "We can't do that. I've had just about all I can stand with big animals' tails."

"Silence!" shouted the Great Kachina. "I'm losing my patience. Do as I say, or I'll erupt the Peaks immediately!"

"Oh no, no, don't do that," Emma Jean said. "We will obtain the hair from Terror the Lion. Will you tell us where he lives?"

"Yes," answered the Great Kachina. "He lives in a large tree west of here. Enough of this. I will give you until tomorrow, or else."

Short gulped and said, "Or else?"

"Yes, or else," boomed the Great Kachina in a loud voice.

At that there was more thunder and lightning and the Great Kachina disappeared.

Short said, "What do you think of that? This is sure scary."

"Never mind that, we must get on with things," Emma Jean said. "Pack up and we will go as quickly as possible to Terror the Lion's lair. We will have to have someone sneak up and grab some hair out of his tail."

Jasper spoke up. "Well, Short should be the one to do that. She is so small, the Lion would probably not notice her."

"Oh, no you don't!" Short cried out. "Not me. I've had enough of this kind of stuff."

"But you did so well with the Bear," all the animals exclaimed.

"I know," said Short, "but I never promised to make a career of grabbing big ferocious animals by the tail. You get someone else to do it. Get Bozo the Hound. He is brave and strong."

Bozo said, "She is right. I'm the one to do it."

"That's agreed, then," said Emma Jean. "Now listen, when we get near to the Lion's den, be real quiet. We will sneak up on tippy toes. Bozo will crawl up to the Lion, and on a count of three, we will all jump up, yelling and screaming at the top of our voices, and then Bozo can grab his tail."

When they arrived at the Lion's lair, sure enough, there he was, sleeping on the limb of a tree. His tail was hanging down and almost reached the ground.

Emma Jean whispered, "Now, here we go. Be as quiet as can be."

They all started to sneak up on the Lion. When they were almost there, the Lion opened one eye. Everybody froze. Pretty soon he closed his eye and apparently was asleep. The whole group advanced. Bozo was waiting for the count of three.

All of a sudden the Lion sprang up and said, "Aha! You thought I was asleep."

Just then he saw Jasper the Rabbit.

"I haven't had a nice young Rabbit for lunch for a long time." He jumped down and snatched up Jasper in his big mouth and sharp teeth and was about to take off.

The lion opened one eye . . .

Short, seeing what a terrible predicament Jasper was in, threw caution to the wind, dashed in, and grabbed the Lion by the tail.

"Yipp!" yelled the Lion, letting loose of Jasper, who promptly disappeared in the bushes. At that time all of the animals let out their particular yells and the Lion took off. When they looked over at Short, they all got a big surprise. There she was with a mouthful of Lion hair. They all went over and gave her kisses and hugs and said, "You did it again, Short. You are so brave."

Short dashed up to the lion and grabbed him by the tail.

Short said, "Who, me? Oh yes, I guess I am," and she gave a little embarrassed laugh. "Tee-hee-hee."

After they had all settled down, Emma Jean said, "Let's go over the hill and get back to the Great Kachina and give him his silly Lion hair."

✧ ✧ ✧

When they returned to Humphreys Peak, the Great Kachina appeared again, accompanied by the same lightning and thunder. But this time the animals were not as frightened.

The voice rang out, "Who goes there and stands before the Great Kachina?"

Short said, "Knock that off. You know who it is."

Emma Jean said, "Shush, shush, we can't afford to get him mad." She spoke to the Great Kachina. "We are the same friends who spoke to you before, and we obtained the hair from the tail of Terror the Lion. So now you must give up your threat of erupting the Peaks."

"Not so fast," shouted the Great Kachina. "One more quest is needed."

"Oh no," said Short. "You are not going to renege and make more requests."

"SILENCE! Yes, you must get some feathers from the Golden Eagle. Do not try to substitute any old Eagle feathers, as I will know because the Golden Eagle's feathers are pure gold. Off with you now,

"The feathers of the Golden Eagle are pure gold . . ."

and do not bother me again until you have the feathers."

With more lightning and thunder, he disappeared.

Short snorted, "He sure likes the bit with the lightning and thunder. What a clown!"

Emma Jean said, "Be careful, he might hear you. We must now plan how we are going to get the golden feathers."

"You are right," said a voice. "The Eagle will be found on the tallest tree in the forest." With more thunder and lightning, they knew it was the Great Kachina.

Short said, "All right, already, will you please cease with the thunder-and-lightning routine? It's killing my ears." So off they went looking for the tallest tree in the forest.

Sandy said, "I will climb to the top of a Pine tree and I will be able to spot the tallest tree." At that, Sandy shot up to the tip of the tree where he was standing. He yelled down, "I see it. It is only a short walk away." He scooted down so fast that he looked like a gray streak.

Emma Jean said, "Now, I don't have to tell you to be quiet. We must sneak up on the Golden Eagle just like we did on the Lion. Who will volunteer to get the feather from the Eagle?" There was a great moment of silence! "Come on now, who is the most qualified? Let's see, someone who can climb trees or who can fly; that narrows it down to Sandy the Squirrel or Herman the Duck."

Sandy said, "Not me. That Eagle could carry me off. I would be so frightened I wouldn't be able to move."

"Well, that settles it. You are the one, Herman," Emma Jean said. "You must fly up and grab a feather."

Herman quacked out, "I can't fly. These wings are just for looks. I'm a tame Duck, not a wild Duck. Only wild Ducks can fly. Look how short my wings are," and he fluttered his wings a little.

Short said, "Come on, Herman, try. Walk up on that small hill and take off. You don't know if you can fly unless you try."

"Oh, all right, here goes!"

At that, he waddled up to the top of a small mound and took off.

Short yelled, "Flap! Flap your wings, Herman, flap."

Herman fell on top of the Eagle, whose golden feathers floated to the ground.

Much to everyone's surprise Herman flew for a few yards, but landed on his beak and slid for several feet. They all ran over and said, "That's great, Herman. We knew that you could do it."

Herman said, "Yes, but I couldn't fly to the top of the tallest tree in the forest."

"Just fly from one limb to another until you get just above the Golden Eagle," said Short, "and then jump down on him, grab a feather and fly to the ground."

"Big deal!" Herman said. "Easy for you, Short, but hard for me."

Emma Jean spoke up, "That's how it must be done. Now we must travel to the tallest tree and then sneak up on the Golden Eagle."

So they quietly approached the tree. When they got there, Emma Jean whispered to Herman, "Here we are. Go do your stuff. Good luck!"

Herman flapped his wings as hard as he could and barely reached the lowest branch. The next one he almost missed completely. The whole group held their breath. Finally, after what seemed forever, he reached a limb that was just above the Golden Eagle, who was having an afternoon nap.

Emma Jean signaled to Herman to fly down upon the Eagle.

Just then poor Herman's foot slipped and he fell awkwardly right on top of the Eagle. The Golden Eagle awoke with a scream, his golden feathers flying in all directions and floating down to the ground. All the animals and Emma Jean ran about and grabbed the golden feathers.

Poor Herman fell and was only able to save himself from harm by getting his wings flapping before he hit the earth.

The Golden Eagle, by this time, was long gone. They all knew that with the supply of feathers they had gathered, this should satisfy the Great Kachina.

Quickly they returned to Humphreys Peak.

"We are here, Great Kachina," shouted Emma Jean. "Now you must grant our petition to stop the Peaks from erupting."

After the usual lightning and thunder, the Great Kachina spoke again. "Not so fast. I have one more quest."

"Oh no," Short said. "Not that again."

There was more thunder, and brighter lightning, and another voice rang out. "George, you let the people go and stop this nonsense about erupting the Peaks."

The Great Kachina meekly said, "Yes, Mother."

The voice continued, "You wait until your father gets home."

Short started to laugh and said, "Goodbye, George!"

At that they all skipped down the road back to the ranch and they lived happily ever after. Now they knew that the San Francisco Peaks would never erupt again.

THE END

Quilliton the Porcupine
Falls in Love

Most animals thought that Quilliton was old and crabby. But actually he was quite young. He appeared older than his age because his quills were not lying smooth but were sticking out in every direction.

When he was a little Porcupine, other Porcupine children would call him "Old Pincushion" and "Crazy Quill" and names like that, and even laughed out loud.

This made him very sad, and he asked his grandfather, "Why are my quills not smooth like the other Porcupine kids in the trees?"

His grandfather laughed and consoled him. "Do not worry. You will find that your quills will serve you very well one of these days."

He thought, "Great for Grandpa to say this," but in the meanwhile he had a hard time getting a date to go eating bark in the trees. As a matter of fact, none of the pretty Porcupine girls would give him the time of day. He would ask very politely, "Would you like to go eat some bark? I know where there are some new Aspen trees. I will be glad to show you where they are."

The Porcupine girls would take one look at his quills and make excuses like, "No thanks, I am not into Aspen trees these days." Quilliton would say, "How about some Oak?"

"No thanks, I can't stand Oak," and then they would walk away with their noses up in the air.

Poor Quilliton would feel so bad. He thought to himself, "I know it is my quills." He would try to brush them, to smooth them down. But as soon as he would stop brushing, *pop* – they would jump up again. "Oh dear," he thought, "I just know that no pretty Porcupine girls will ever be interested in me."

This is why he became kind of grumpy. Whenever anyone tried to be pleasant to him, he would think, "I know they are just trying to be nice so they can make fun of my quills when my back is turned."

Now, this was not true. Many of the older Porcupines thought he was quite handsome. They knew that he was very kind-hearted and dependable and good to his parents.

As a matter of fact, whenever Quilliton would come across a nice sweet bit of bark on a Pine tree, he would clip it with his teeth and then bring it to his mother. She would thank him for being such a good boy, but all the time she was talking, she would be trying to brush down his quills, hoping that Quilliton wouldn't notice. "It is no use, Mother. My quills will always be like that. I am just going to have to live with it," he would say.

So Quilliton grew into a very big and strong Porcupine. One of the reasons was, he would choose bark that was low in cholesterol. He always chewed his food thoroughly and never gulped it down.

He was quite content, but thought that he would always remain a bachelor.

One day he saw something. He couldn't believe

his eyes. A most beautiful sight. It was the prettiest Porcupine girl he could imagine. There she was—her quills were nice and smooth, lying just perfectly, and her pink nose was tilted just enough to give her an air of regality. Her feet and toes were so delicate and feminine and her nails looked like she had just polished them. She had just the right kind of Pine tree perfume.

Quilliton's heart jumped. It went *bang bang* against his chest. He was afraid that she would hear it and ask if he was being a drum or something.

Although he felt that he would be rejected, he knew that he just had to ask her to go to the spring animal festival. Edging toward her, he mumbled, "I know you won't go to the festival with—I mean—will you go to the me—that is, how about a date to go to the festival?"

He heard another voice: "That's right, Priscilla babe. How about swinging with me at the animal hoedown?"

He turned around and sure enough, it was Beauregard, the handsome young Porcupine that all the girls flipped over.

Priscilla said, "Oh, Beauregard, do you mean little ol' me?"

"Right on there, chick. Let's go and show the world how to cut a rug. I'll teach you the Porcupine twist."

So off they went, leaving poor Quilliton feeling sad. "Oh well," he thought. "I'm used to this kind of treatment. At least I tried."

By this time you must be aware that Porcupines eat bark. Sometimes they get carried away and eat all around the tree in a circle. This is called girdling the tree. Unfortunately, this causes the tree to die, making the forest rangers very unhappy. Their job is to see that the trees grow straight and tall, to protect them so they can be harvested and then cut up into lumber for houses to be built.

They did not mind the Porcupines until they became too numerous. So one day Jake the forest ranger came to see Papa Bader to get his advice on what to do about the Porcupine population. He was upset and said that unless something was done about this problem, the forest might be ruined.

Papa Bader calmed him down and said, "Let's see what we can do about this. Of course, you must not shoot them or use a cruel steel trap. I will show you how you can trap them humanely, and then they can be moved to another part of the woods."

"We will make a figure-four trap. This will catch the Porcupines without hurting them." He drew a picture of how it should be constructed.

"To catch Porcupines we must bait the trap with a tender young tree branch soaked in salt. They love salt. When one of them crawls under the box and starts to gnaw on the branch and pull on it, the figure-four slips off and down comes the box — *slam* — and the animal is caught without any harm. Then a board can be slipped under the box and the animal can be removed to another part of the forest and released."

"This is a fine idea," said forest ranger Jake. So together they made the trap and placed it in the forest.

Not long after, Beauregard and Priscilla came walking in the area where the trap had been set. They had become fast friends. If the truth were known, they were going steady. Priscilla thought that Beauregard was so handsome and really had a crush on him. She was so enamored with his looks that she didn't give one thought to his character.

When they saw the trap and the delicious branch within, Beauregard said, "You go first, my dear," pretending that he was just being polite. But really he was afraid that it might be a trap. Priscilla, who believed anything Beauregard said, replied, "Oh thank you. You are so gallant," and walked right into the trap. She took a bite on the stick and *bang*, down came the box. She found herself in complete darkness.

She was in a panic and shouted out to Beauregard, "Save me, save me." But just then someone let out a terrible scream. It was Robert the Bobcat.

Now, Bobcats, or Lynx, are the only predators that can kill a Porcupine. They accomplish this by flipping the Porcupine over on its back. This enables them to avoid the quills and at the same time attack their unprotected underside. (This doesn't make Bobcats all bad. You know that they have to eat, too, and nature has given them this skill so they can survive.)

Porcupines are deathly afraid of Bobcats, so when Beauregard heard this scream, he forgot all about Priscilla, ran for the nearest tree, and scrambled up as fast as he could. Robert the Bobcat, catching the scent of Priscilla in the trap, ran over and tried to break in to capture poor, helpless Priscilla.

Now, unknown to everyone involved in this little drama, Quilliton had been watching this for some time. He would never ever think of interfering with Priscilla and Beauregard's courtship. He was too much of a gentleman to do that. But when he saw Robert the Bobcat go for the trap that held his only true love, he knew he had to do something to save her.

He hurried up to Robert, and a very strange and wonderful thing happened. All of the quills that had appeared so strange and funny to so many others arose, sticking out in all directions. They were a formidable sight. No matter which angle Robert attacked, there were those wonderful quills menacing him. Finally, when he caught a full smack in the nose from Quilliton's tail, he turned and fled.

Quilliton hurried over to the wooden trap and with his sharp teeth tore a hole large enough to liberate Priscilla. When she saw who had rescued her and noticed Beauregard up the tree, she said, "Quilliton, you are so brave. You are my hero," and she gave him a Porcupine kiss, which, of course, is rubbing noses.

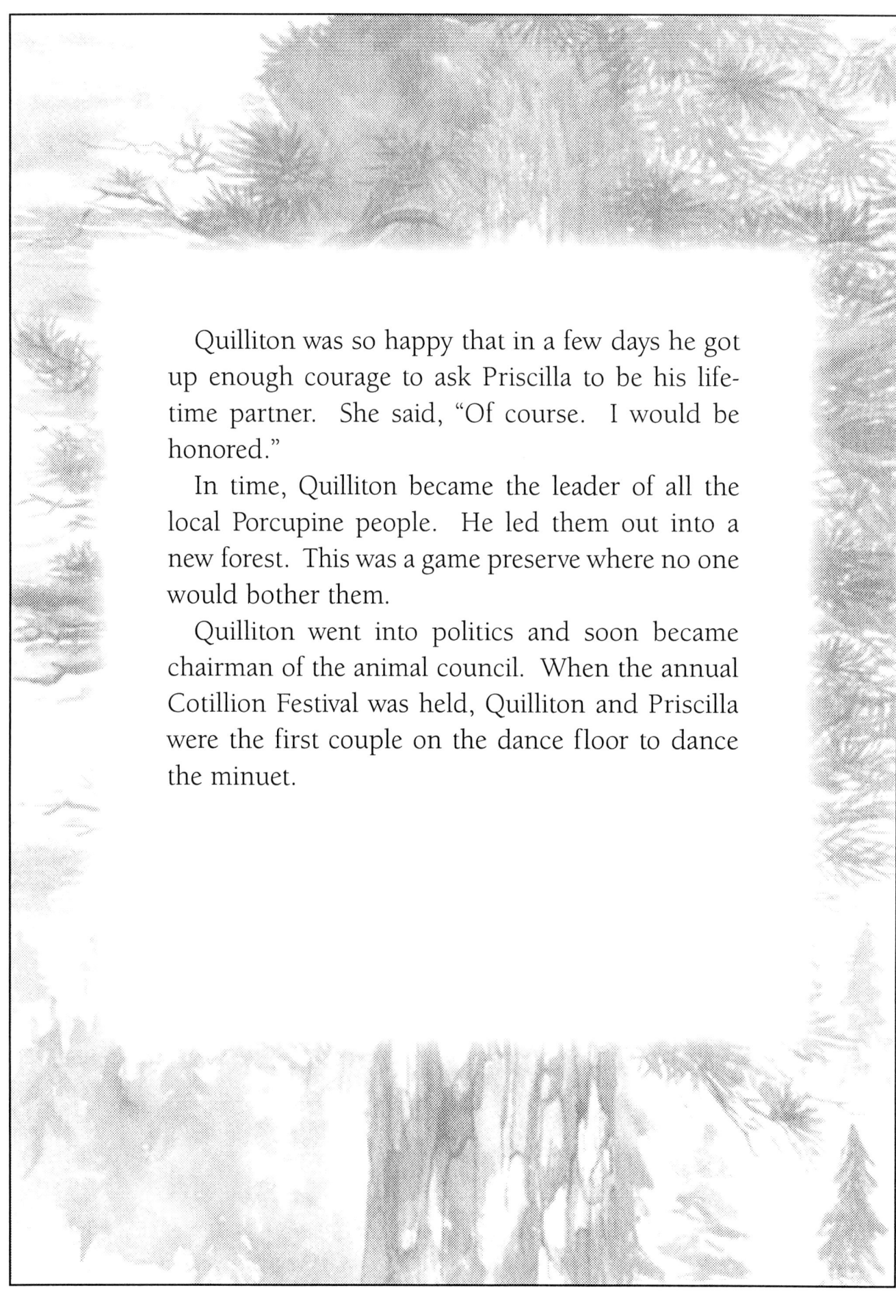

Quilliton was so happy that in a few days he got up enough courage to ask Priscilla to be his lifetime partner. She said, "Of course. I would be honored."

In time, Quilliton became the leader of all the local Porcupine people. He led them out into a new forest. This was a game preserve where no one would bother them.

Quilliton went into politics and soon became chairman of the animal council. When the annual Cotillion Festival was held, Quilliton and Priscilla were the first couple on the dance floor to dance the minuet.

THE END

About the Author

Lou Bader's career has spanned a cross-section of the arts: A professional singer on radio and stage; a television personality and movie director/producer (*The Magnificent Mullato*); a producer and director at the Pasadena Playhouse, the Burbank Civic Light Opera and the Glendale Light Opera; a sculptor in bronze; and more recently an author.

He has also been a building contractor, realtor, aircraft designer and county commissioner. A subdivision near the lovely San Francisco Peaks in Flagstaff was created by the artist and bears his name — Baderville.

The Great Kachina is his second book; the first was *In the Shadow of the San Francisco Peaks,* a collection of his experiences of pioneer life in northern Arizona.

Although he was born in Cincinnati, Ohio, Bader was raised in the rugged logging town of Flagstaff, Arizona, which gave him an early respect for animals and all living creatures. This affinity is evident in the details of his bronze animal sculptures as well as his writing. *The Great Kachina* portrays animals with personalities and feelings, interacting with human beings. With this book he enters the new territory of children's literature.